Sarah Dana Greenough

Mary Magdalene

A Poem

Sarah Dana Greenough

Mary Magdalene
A Poem

ISBN/EAN: 9783744771276

Printed in Europe, USA, Canada, Australia, Japan

Cover: Foto ©Andreas Hilbeck / pixelio.de

More available books at **www.hansebooks.com**

MARY MAGDALENE

A POEM

BY

⸌MRS. RICHARD⸍ GREENOUGH

AUTHOR OF ARABESQUES

MEMBER OF THE SOCIETY OF THE ARCADIA, AND OF THE ROYAL
ACADEMY OF ST. CECILIA, OF ROME

BOSTON
JAMES R. OSGOOD AND COMPANY
1880

TO MY HUSBAND

I AFFECTIONATELY INSCRIBE THIS POEM,

SUGGESTED BY HIS STATUE OF

MARY MAGDALENE

AT THE TOMB.

Palazzo della Congregazione,
367 Via Nazionale, Rome.

NOTE.

AMONG the ancient Greeks and Romans, when the celestial divinities were invoked, the suppliant stood with uplifted arms; in addressing the terrestrial deities, the arms were extended forward; and in imploring the infernal powers, the arms were directed downward.

Part First.

I.

Twas night: upon Jerusalem the moon
Poured her still splendours down; the purple sky,
Embossed with silver stars, majestic spread
Its quivering canopy to meet the dim
And distant circle of th' horizon's bound
In shadowy hills, and gleaming, half-seen plains,
The plains that wait, the hills that watch around
The rock-clasped pomp of great Jerusalem.
Fair rose the city from its mighty belt
Of dark and rough-hewn walls: its palaces

B

Crowded in sculptured pride, its synagogues,
Its storied colonnades, its myriad roofs,
Its terraced gardens fringed with ancient trees,
Shone glittering in the rain of lucent rays;
And in the midst the marvel of the land,
The giant Golden Temple, upward soared,
Far flashing through the stillness of the night.

II.

Silent the city slept, but on the verge
Of the sheer precipice, stood glimmering white,
'Mid slender cypresses and towering palms,
A stately marble pile, whose pillared porch
And wide-oped windows, all ablaze with light,
Proclaimed the revelry that reigned within.
It was the home of Mary Magdalene,
The beautiful and the unholy one,
The Magdalene, that sinful city's boast,
The Magdalene, that sacred city's shame.

III.

On this soft summer night the high-born crowd

Which formed her customed court was gathered there :

The thick-browed Jews with cold and cruel glance,

And full, red lips, within whose deep curves lurked

Sarcastic lines of brooding discontent,

Hardening their sensuousness with underchord

Of bitter, biting hate ; their ample robes

Of purple and fine linen folded close

Around their sinewy frames ; unheeding all

Their ancient rules, pressed thither.   Pliant Greeks,

Vivid and mobile, panther-like in grace,

As serpents wily and as falcons keen,

Their chiselled features flashing with the play

Of their astute discourse, enamelled o'er

With apt quotation from their country's bards,

Inwrought with sophistries, dank poison dew

Of unbelief dark tinging every thought,   .

Clustered within those flower-scented halls.

In gay-fringed robes draped with well-studied art,

Their golden circlets gleaming on their arms,

Their dainty locks perfumed with Orient spice,

They delicately smiled, and subtly sneered

In the sweet accents of their native tongue.

The young patricians of imperial Rome,

Their haughty heads set on unbending necks,

Their very courtesy tainted with command,

Their slowly moving eyes and level lids,

Their swollen nostrils, and their flaccid cheeks

Telling the tale of drear satiety;

Their massive shoulders and their brawny chests

Showing athwart the costly broidered folds

That wrapt them in their pomp of sullen pride,

Sought in that chosen dwelling of delight

To turn their memories from the feasts of Rome.

IV.

These, her companions and her courtiers, lay

Within her sumptuous banquet room, their forms

Outstretched on downy couches round the board

Heaped high with luscious viands brought from far,

From east and west, from north and glowing south,

To tempt the pampered appetites they fed.

Bright glancing wines in precious vases poured

Their rich aromas on the tepid air,

While round the hall huge scented torches burned,

Their tall flames flickering in the fitful breeze

That swayed above the city's hush of sleep.

The smooth mosaic pavement was o'erstrewn

With scattered flowers, jessamine and rose,

And music stole forth ever and anon,

Filling the pauses of the jocund talk

With cadence mirthful or with murmurous plaint.

V.

High throned upon her carven ivory couch

Upheld by golden lions, silent lay

The Magdalene, the queen of that choice court,

And listened, listless, to the shifting flow

Of sparkling jest and wit-embroidered speech;
But when the singers' voices thrilled the air,
She raised her wistful lids and gazed afar
As though her soul were stirring in its sleep,
Nor knew the life that lapped her day by day,
But solitary dreamed in realms apart.
Her soft, white limbs revealed by silvery gauze
Through which their lustrous tints like moonlight shone,
The waves of rippling gold that crowned her small
And languid-leaning head, her violet eyes
That dewy swam beneath their deep-fringed lids,
Now careless resting on her gathered guests,
Now bent upon the flower-scattered floor;
The rose-blush of her childlike, dimpled mouth,
Its corners drooping with a faint distaste;
The witching rhythm of harmonious grace
Controlling every youthful curve and line;
On these enticing charms the torches shed
Their bright illumination;—but not these
Alone their radiance showed. Around that sweet

And melting beauty hovered in the air

A strange, peculiar spell,—a magic art

Some of her courtiers deemed it,—which had might

To set the stamp of innocence upon

That lovely and that too belovèd face.

No brazen stare of conscious guilt confessed

The inner aching of a shame-pierced soul,

No glance of florid blandishment proclaimed

The loss of all that woman holds most dear,

No flippant laughter parted those young lips

To echo heartless through the sumptuous hall,

No word of plague-struck meaning dropped its taint

Companioning the jests around her board ;

Unlike all others of her sinful caste,

As a white rose 'mid flaunting tulips seen,

The far-famed Magdalene lay silent there,

Her every beauty beaming fair revealed,

Yet haloed by her own unconsciousness.

VI.

Now as she listless dreamed, her ear was caught

By sudden harshness in the tones of one

Who seldom spoke, a swarthy, gray-haired Jew.

A shadowed frown disturbed the level line

Of her sweet brows, as the discordant voice

Came rasping on the warm and scented air.

" A beggarly impostor, nothing more;

One of the spawn of ignorance and craft

That swarms upon us in these latter days,

Leading the stupid multitude astray:

Soon to be smitten by the very hands

That now applaud, to be reviled and cursed

By the capricious voices that to-day

Proclaim him as the great Messiah come.

Most fortunate the cunning villain is

If these dear friends and followers, undeceived,

Turn not to rend him quivering, limb from limb;

Forestalling the quick day when Roman hands

Shall mete out Roman justice to his crime."

He seized a crystal cup and drained it dry,

Then set it down so roughly that the tall

And twisted stem was shivered in his grasp.

VII.

A youthful Roman knight, a stranger there,

Who was in act of raising to his lips

A rubied nectarine from the broad vase

Of fretted gold that stood beside his arm,

Turned his calm look upon the hoary Jew,

And quiet answered, "I have yet to learn

What crime may lurk in teachings such as those

Myself have heard from him thou thus contemn'st.

Last week as I was travelling hither, near

The hostel where I tarried for the night,

This cunning villain, as thou call'st him, stood

And taught the wondering multitude his faith.

As in the hostel not a soul was left,

But all had crowded thither, I too went

To see what novel folly moved them thus.

I stood and listened.   Cavil as thou wilt,

He spoke as never mortal spoke before!"

VIII.

A burst of laughter loud its greeting gave `

To the young Roman's words.   The elder knight

Who had companioned there his kinsman, bent

His mocking gaze upon him, and besought

He would not stint such unaccustomed fare,

But generously share with all the guests

The wondrous teachings of this latest fool.

With haughty glance the young patrician scanned

The eager, jeering faces round the board,

And slow replied, "I doubt me if the words

This peasant spoke, could find an entrance here.

He told of truth and purity and good :

He taught God is a spirit, and as such
Must worshipped be 'in spirit, and in life
Of noble deeds, of love from man to man;
Counting no cost too great to win that pearl
Of price, the spirit's holiness." He paused
And looked around upon the silent throng.

IX.

His circling glance fell on the Magdalene.
Half raised upon her rounded arm she leaned,
Bent forward in a line of wavy grace;
Her golden head inclined to catch his words,
Her eyes attentive fixed upon his face,
With parted lips she listened from her couch.
Sudden before that loveliness all thought
Of the poor peasant faded from the mind
Of the young Roman. "How divinely fair
The woman is! No marvel that her fame
Has passed the far gates of imperial Rome.
How exquisite her posture! What delight

To lavish kisses on those deep-fringed lids !"
But as he speechless gazed, her eyes looked forth
Mutely imploring, and her low voice came
With mild entreaty, " Probus, is there more ?"
And with the instant habit of command
Learned from his Stoic tutor, pressing down
The quick desires high-foaming in his heart,
Obedient to her will, he spoke again.
"The people thronged about him as he taught,
    And listened stirless; while the slow tears ran
    Down many a rugged cheek, and women sobbed
    When he, uplifting both his arms, thus cried;
'Oh ye, my weary ones, behold your rest!
    Lay down your burden, lay it on my neck,
    And I will bear it for you.   Cast aside
    Your sins: learn love and holiness and peace!'"
The stranger ceased.   For some brief moments' space
An unaccustomed silence brooded round;
Then, as if shaking off unwelcome thought,
Gay jest and jocund laughter reigned anew.

X.

As one who hearkens wondering to some strain

Of novel harmonies, nor can descry

The fulness of the meaning of those sweet

Far-reaching modulations, but perplexed

And baffled, seeks in vain to seize some clue

To guide him through their beauteous labyrinth,

The Magdalene had listened to the words

Of the young knight ; and now, neglected all

Her customed court of ardent worshippers,

Soft as a snowflake from her couch she slid,

And o'er the rose-strewn pavement gliding slow,

In silence vanished through the sculptured door.

XI.

Across the threshold of her chamber passed

The Magdalene with inward look intent,

Nor stayed her onward step, nor glanced upon

The flower-crowned altar and the marble form

Of Aphrodite smiling from her niche,

The silver bed by laughing loves upheld,

Thick strewn with rose leaves its cerulean folds,

The alabaster vases in whose cups

Their perfumed lamps were burning to diffuse

A dreamy twilight through the softened room;

These she passed by unheeding, and toward

The broad and open balcony moved on,

And there she paused.   Below, the garden lay,

And from above the quiet moon shone down.

But on the lovely brow of Magdalene

Hovered a strange unrest.   With claspèd hands

She stood and gazed upon the shades beneath,

Then turned her deep look upward to the skies,

While new and vague emotions trembled o'er

The fair, transparent mirror of her face.

XII.

Vainly she sought to read the meaning right

Of that strange tale the Roman knight had told.

Like to a wandering wave-borne leaf, her thought
Lay floating helpless on the heaving sea
Before her untaught powers, till fatigue
Vanquished her wavering efforts, and she turned
To rest her mind upon the well-known past.
Her childish life rose up before her, far
By the blue waves of the Corinthian gulf,
Her gentle mother in their cottage home
Beneath the vine-clad hill, her father's voice
Of greeting glad, when from his vessel's side
He called his welcome to them as they stood
And laughed for joy to see his face again,—
That alien Jewish father with his name
Barneh of Magdala. And then she saw
Her youthful mother dying, and again
She heard her mournful wail, " My precious one !
Ah woe is me, thou art so beautiful !"
And then she saw the white-robed priests who came,
Her mother dead, and carried her away
Unto the gorgeous temple glittering fair

With sculptures, glowing with resplendent hues
On its rich-pictured walls.   There wealth of flowers
Made odorous the air that pulsed beneath
The weight melodious of sweet songs breathed forth ,
By fresh young voices, hymning high the praise
Of foam-born Aphrodite; while the porch
Stood widely open to invite the crowd
Of worshippers who changeful filled the fane,
Bringing rich gifts in joyous homage laid
Upon the hundred altars that between
The shining ranks of leafy columns white
Stood ready to receive their offerings.

XIII.

There had she passed her days of early youth,
There learned to chant the ringing odes of praise,
To strike the sounding cithern, and to weave
The graceful circles of the mystic dance
That daily imaged to the fringing crowd
The worship of the goddess whom she served.

There had she lived, caressed and praised by all
Who ministered beneath the temple roof,
Proclaimed the favourite priestess of the shrine ;
While gifts more costly than all others brought
Were laid upon the altars by the hands
Of those whose lips pressed kisses on her feet.

XIV.

Till that dread day when, bursting through the crowd
Of wine-flushed votaries and flower-crowned priests
Around her as she led the mystic dance,
Her father, long unseen, had made his way,
And seized her by the arm, and impious words
Dishonouring the deity, had shrieked.
And then the tumult and the angry cries
And threatening gestures, that had made her swoon
Upon the floor with chill and anguished fright.
And then again she saw the haggard face
Of that dear father as he bent above

c

Her couch that night and whispered, "Come with me,
My daughter; flee from this accursèd place
And come with me !"   Again she followed on
Through the dark corridors and vacant halls,
Until they stood without; then made their way
Unto the rocking boat that bore them thence
Across the waves.   Again she saw his face
Show white and ghastly in the early dawn.
Poison had tipped the 'dagger's point which deep
Into his side had pierced in that fierce fray
With Aphrodite's raging priests; and thus
He died, imploring with his latest breath
That to Judea she would flee, nor make
Again her home within those temple walls
Whence he had ransomed her at well spent cost
Of his own life.

XV.

Why did her father loathe
And dread that gorgeous temple where each day

Passed in rejoicing dances, and in song?

Why did he call the priests accursed who taught

Her and her young companions how to please?

Sacred was Aphrodite.   Were not all

Her high behests to be obeyed with joy?

And yet her father had blasphemed that name

With words of direst hatred.—Then he held

Another faith ;—perchance his faith was true!

What was that faith?   How should she know the truth?

And he, this peasant teacher, he whose words

Had stirred such vague disquiet in her mind,

What did he mean when he besought that throng

To seek for love and holiness and peace?

Surely he meant some other love from that

Which had been taught her in the far-off fane.

And holiness—the word she did not know—

And peace, oh yes, she could imagine peace,

It must be that she longed for, but in vain.

Anew the misty veil of troubled thought

Floated across her youthful face, anew

She gazed up to the distant sky, as though
Seeking its answer to her questionings.

XVI.

At length she turned and called to her the guard
Who kept his watch beside her chamber door,
And forth upon the terrace came the form
Of a tall Nubian slave.   His ebon chest
And sinewy arms dark shone like polished bronze,
His yellow vest was cinctured with broad gold,
A short two-edgèd sword beside him hung;
And in a leash of twisted silver led,
A tawny hunting leopard flecked with black,
Followed with head low bent and stealthy tread.
" Go to the stranger Probus : say to him
That I await him here."   The slave passed thence
With homage reverential; and again
The Magdalene gazed upward to the sky
And softly whispered, " holiness and peace !"

XVII.

A step impatient crossed the chamber floor,

And close beside her stood the Roman knight,

Flushed and expectant. Eagerly he caught

Her hand, and on its yielding velvet pressed

His hurried kisses. Gently from his clasp

The hand was drawn, and her calm voice outbreathed,

" Not so, O Probus ; not for this I called

Thee to my side. To-night I worship not,

Nor honour Aphrodite. I would ask

Of thee alone, if thou canst answer me,

Some question that myself I cannot solve."

" Speak, beauteous one," thus Probus, " speak, and I

Will answer as I may thy questionings ;

But say not that to-night thou wilt not pay

Due homage to the goddess !" And his look

Scanned the young charms that lay beneath her robe

Of silvery gauze, and revelled in the sight.

" Words thou hast spoken that disturb my breast,"
She slowly answered, "and I fain would learn
The meaning that they hold.   I know of peace
In part, not wholly ; but, what is that love
Of which the peasant told them ?   I was taught
In the Corinthian fane, 'twas love to fill
The cup of joy to all who yearned to taste.
But this he cannot mean.   That cup of joy
Grows heavy in my hands, my shrinking lips
Are weary of its taste.   It gives no peace.
And holiness—how sweet the word—I know
Its meaning not, but yet I love the sound :
Tell me, O Probus, what is holiness ?"

XVIII.

A mocking flicker gleamed within the eyes
Of the young knight.   "Oh thou fair cozening snake !"
He mentally exclaimed, "how deep the art
They taught thee in bright Corinth !"   Then he spoke,

His proud lip curving with sarcastic scorn.

" It is a Jewish word, a Jewish thing,

Unmeet for such warm lips as these, unfit

For harbour in this soft and snowy breast.

The priests in gladsome Corinth taught thee well.

Thou hast no need for other faith than this,

To scatter pleasure where thy light feet tread,

To joy in all that life and youth can give,

To worship Venus, and due honour pay

To all her voice proclaims as fair and good."

He closer drew, and round her supple form

He clasped his nervous arm.   She heeded not,

But gazed afar with wistful dreamy eyes.

The night wind brought the odours from below,

Faint and delicious, an enchanted hush

Deep wrapt the sleeping garden.   Bending down

His head, he looked into her moonlit face;

And as he looked, he saw her rose-lips move,

And heard her murmur, " holiness and peace !"

XIX.

"O Magdalene, my lovely one," he prayed,
"Hast thou no word, no look to give to me?
Thou needest not these arts of coy delay.
See how the flowers gently droop their heads,
And rest upon each other in sweet sleep;
See how the moonlight's silvery kiss is prest
Upon the tender grass and bending shrubs;
See, all invites to love! Behold, I sue
E'en at thy feet—I never knelt before,
My Magdalene, fill up to me the cup,
The mantling cup of joy: delay no more!"
Sadly she turned her golden head and looked
On the impassioned suitor at her feet.
"Probus," she said, "thou art not like to those
Who crowd around me in Jerusalem.
I felt a new and potent strength within
Thy words to-night when, braving the rude scorn
Of my ill-mannered guests, thou didst unfold

Strange doctrines spoken by that peasant poor.

Behold, I have no friend. I dimly feel

There is a something better than this life

Which I have led till now. A vague unrest

Torments me, and faint whisperings in the air

Come to disquiet me with shadowy hopes

And painful thrilling fears. Something there is

That lies beyond the circle of my days.

My faith was not my father's faith, for he

Abhorred great Aphrodite. How shall I,

O Probus, search the mystery within

My breast? How learn what the unknown may be

That calls me with its half-heard tones, and stirs

Such longing and disquiet in my heart?"

XX.

As the pure voice its low complaining spoke,

Made eloquent by earnest pleading eyes,

Sincere and truthful, through the knight there sped

A dart of keen conviction. This was truth!

No artful weaving of a shameless net
To snare him more securely in her toils.
His mind, well trained in the great schools of Greece,
Could follow in its course her troubled thought.
Within the famed hetaira's breast he found
A blind and struggling soul that vainly longed
For light, for truth. And with this thought there
    came
A rush of tenderness within his heart,
Tempering the sensual fire that had burned
At sight of her, unsoftened until now.
All that was best and noblest in him drew
With sudden impulse toward that lovely one;
So sinful and so sinless ! To possess
Her love became the hunger of his heart.
"Say, Probus, canst thou help ?" With hands out-
    stretched,
Her sweet face anxiously she bent on him,
As one who pleads for a most precious boon.

XXI.

He rose, and mastering his throbbing will,

Calmly he spoke. "Yes, Magdalene, I know

All thou dost seek to learn."—A flash of joy

With quick irradiation lit her look.—

" O child, thou deemest thou hast learnt the lore

Of love, for so those false priests taught thee; but

Love's secret lies beyond. Not joy of sense

Alone is love : love is that finer thought

That does inform the deeper soul of man

With keen desire for another soul,

In which its hunger for the beautiful

Shall find at last its sweet and longed-for food.

Such is the love thou needest, Magdalene.

E'en as thy form, thy soul is beautiful ;

It craves for union with another soul,

And solitary mourns its lonely lot.

Listen, belovèd one, and I will teach

A deeper lore than any thou hast learnt.

Give to my soul thine own, and thou shalt know
What the great gods' best gift to man has been.
The still closed petals of thy heart shall ope
As flowers open to the sun's soft light.
The vague disquiet of thy breast shall melt
As clouds of night before day's tender dawn.
Come to my arms; there shalt thou find thy rest,
Thy every hope, thy every dream fulfilled!"
Earnest his deep tones thrilled upon the air,
Fervent the look he bent upon her face.
She stilly spoke; " But, Probus, I would learn
Of holiness : thou teachest but of love!"

XXII.

A sudden whirl of burning passion swept
Throughout his frame.   He smote upon his brow
With his clenched hand.   " Thrice cursèd fool was I
To tell thee of this prating Nazarene!
What are his words to thee?   Thou know'st not him,
Nor ever will know.   That man loves thee not :

He cannot love thee, being what thou art.

The holiness thou seekest is a bar

For ever raised between thy soul and his.

But I—I love thee, branded as thou art

By pious scorn : I love thee, Magdalene !

Give me thy love, and I will bear thee hence,

And 'mid the splendours of imperial Rome

Will live for thee, will love but thee alone !"

He caught her in his eager arms, and pressed

Devouring kisses on her rippling hair,

Her brow, her cheek, her lips.   With faint, low cry

She tore herself away, and through the gloom

Fled like a shadowy vision from his view.

XXIII.

Silent he stood.   The great veins in his throat

Sent crowding currents to his surging brain.

The moonlight streamed upon the grassy lawns,

A bird sang softly in the midnight hush,

A faint breeze stirred the branches of the trees.

Slowly his calm returned.   A bitter smile

Wreathed his stern lips.   " A whim, a passing whim ! "

He sneering muttered.   " She is like her kind.

As clouds upon the wind-tormented sky

Their fancies come and go.—She pines for Greece.

An alien in this harsh, barbaric land,

She longs again for Corinth, and the gay

And flower-scented pleasures of her days .

In that, her early home.—It were as wise

To plant an acorn in a fountain's cup,

And look to see it grow, as to believe

This change from all she has been, to a life

That deals with problems such as these her sick

And yearning fancy broods on to my cost.

But she will change again ; and I can wait.

No Vestal art thou, Mary Magdalene ! "

Part Second.

I.

THE sun shone bright on great Jerusalem
Proud towering from the plain. Toward her gates,
Covering the winding roads and hill-side paths,
Came crowding on a mighty multitude.
The Passover with solemn summons called
All pious Jews within those sacred walls,
There to rejoice together that the Lord
Had smitten down their cruel enemy
In ancient times; had wrung old Egypt's heart
With anguish for the death of its best loved,

And so had set his chosen people free !
Gray-headed sires leaning on their staves,
And little children with short tottering steps,
And stalwart fathers with their sun-browned wives,
Their youthful daughters and their hardy sons,
Each bearing wallet or some scanty scrip,
Or leading fleecy lamblings for the feast ;
Toiled on toward the consecrated gates.
Broad, heavy chariots, drawn by oxen dight
With gaudy trappings, leaning wide apart,
Patient, with plodding tread, pursued their path ;
And covered litters curtained close, upborne
By half-stripped forms of panting servants, blocked
The life-encumbered ways ; while horsemen wound
Amid the journeying throngs, and frequent droves
Of the meek beasts foredoomed to sacrifice,
And camels turning vicious, sidelong looks,
Their tall necks rising high above the crowd,
Their round humps laden with vast wicker crates
Holding the terrified and heaped-up doves

That rigid Jewish rites demanded, mixed
In one inextricable mass beneath
The frowning city walls.   Still on they poured
From morn till low the sun began to sink,   ʼ
And scattered grew the groups, and faint the sounds
That had throughout the long day beat the air.

II.

But then came hurrying to the gate that looked
Toward Bethany dark nestling 'neath its trees,
Fleet messengers who, breathless entering, spread
Their tidings through the city.   On the hill
Appeared a serried mass ; and from the gate
Outburst in crowding waves a multitude,
With joyous cries and high uplifted palms
Their greeting greenly waving.   Nearer came
The dense procession through the sunset sheen ;
And shouts of triumph rang, and chanted song,
ʼ " Hosanna to the Son of David, King !
Hosanna to the great Messiah, come

D

To save God's chosen people, and to lead
Them forth to victory!"   And as they drew
Closer, the dark mass opened, and was seen
One riding on a meek and snow-white ass
Which gently trode along the green-strewn way
As though it loved the burden that it bore.
And as the multitude, come forth to meet
Their great Messiah, gazed upon that One,
A look of reverent wonder slowly fell
Upon all faces, with accordant awe.

III.

Clad in a robe of coarse and dark-hued wool
Girded about him with a leathern cord,
Upon his feet rough sandals, travel worn,
The Jewish Prophet looked a Heaven-born King!
Calm on his smooth, broad brow, command sate throned,
His clear, full opened eye with powerful glance
Seemed through the secrets of each heart to pierce
With vision supernaturally keen,

Yet filled with a compassion all divine.

Supremest peace its stamp sublime had pressed

On those firm-moulded lips, which wordless breathed

The inspiration of immortal love.

A solemn joy, an awful tenderness

Rayed forth from that still face ; while silence spread

A pulsing hush around him, as the waves

Of human life, wide parting, swayed aside

In act of homage, as the Prophet came.

IV.

Beneath a shadowy olive tree beside

The crowded way, there stood a sight full fair,

Which on another day had drawn the gaze

Of all the curious crowd ; yet now unmarked.

Close guarded by a band of armèd slaves.

Their scarlet tunics blazing in the sun,

A sumptuous litter carved with rarest skill,

Mother of pearl and gold, upon the necks

Of its strong bearers rested.   On its height

Of rosy, pearl-embroidered cushions lay ·
The graceful form of Mary Magdalene,
Daintily sheltered from the westering rays
By canopy of peacock feathers wove,
Clad in pale azure robes of Grecian fold,
Whence gleamed her snow-white arms and jewelled
And crowned with wreathing braids of golden hair.

V.

Since that first day when on her listening ear
Had come the tidings of the lowly One
Who taught the people doctrines strange and new,
And promised to the weary-hearted, rest;
She had with constant effort sought to know
More of this latest Prophet.   When each night
Around her costly banquet gathered all
Her wonted court, attentively she bent
Her hearing to each word that spoke of him.
And day by day more constantly her guests
Of this new Teacher told.   With bitter scorn

The Pharisees reproached his unbelief
Of all their law held sacred; called him brand
Of hell-fire cast within their temple walls,
Which, not extinguished, would consume them all
In the destruction of their ancient faith.
The mocking Greeks sneered at his lofty aim
To curb the headstrong impulses of man,
Holding a standard up which gods themselves
Might well despair of reaching. Romans smiled
In cold contempt as at an alien feud
Betwixt two parties in a subject state,
Which they could crush at will. But no one spoke
Such words as Probus, since unseen, had said
When he, that Teacher's words repeating, filled
Her heart with wistful thoughts. Then summoning ,
The trustiest of her slaves, the Nubian,
She sent him forth to seek among the throngs
Crowding the temple and each market-place,
For tidings of that One. And he brought back
Stories most strange. The blind beheld the light

At his command, the fevered sick were healed,
The life-long palsied stood upon their feet,
And at his word the buried dead arose !

VI.

She bade him back to ask if Jesus were
Mild, gentle in his tones, compassionate
Of visage ; whether hate and scorn for those
Who knew him not abode within his breast.
For since the scathing words of Probus fell
Upon her ear, her timid heart had failed
Beneath the burden of a formless fear.
" Why was it that this Prophet would not deign
To give to her the love he taught that man
Owed to his fellow-man ?   What was the bar
That holiness had raised for aye between
His soul and hers ?   And what that holiness ?
And why for ever ?   What did Probus know
About the life beyond the dreadful Styx ?
In the Elysian fields perchance her soul

Might meet with his o'er plains of asphodel

Slow gliding on, with light immortal crowned :

And he might look on her, and might caress

With gentle hand her lowly bended head ;

Might smile upon her in that spirit land

Within whose bounds no shadowy bar might be !"

VII.

Then from his quest the messenger returned.

" The Prophet hated and contemned alone

The Pharisees and hypocrites who robbed

Widows and orphans of their scanty crust,

Pretexting tribute for the temple, where

The Scribes sate, vexing sore the patient poor

With imposts heavy and most hard to bear.

On these he poured forth fierce, indignant scorn,

And scourged with wrathful words until they slunk

Silently cowering thence like beaten hounds,

But to all others he was ever mild.

He fed the hungry who around him stood

Forgetful of their need, the while they hung

Upon his words ; he pitied all who mourned.

He called young children to him, on his knees

He held their wondering forms, and bade his friends

Learn of their meekness and their purity ;

Warning them as those children to become

If they would enter that great kingdom's gates

Whereof he came to tell."—She sate in thought.—

" Then purity was there ; a child was pure

Leading its childlike life.   Her life was not

Like to a child's life of unconscious days.

Could purity and holiness be one ?"

VIII.

And so she dwelt in silent questionings.

A spiritual hunger daily grew

Within her breast, a longing vast and vague ;

An aspiration to a something high

Above all she had known ; until this day

Her slave had tidings brought that e'er the night

Jesus of Nazareth, the Prophet, would

Enter the walls of great Jerusalem.

And she had thither come, and waited long,

Fearing to lose her timorous hope, to see

The Prophet as he passed upon his way

Unnoting her, who smitten with the dread

That seeing her and hating her were one,

Because of that strange holiness which raised

Its unknown bar between her soul and his,

Lay in her pomp of beauty, with her heart

Fast beating 'neath her gorgeous canopy.

IX.

At last the Nubian, from the hillock where

He stood and watched, came hurrying to her side.

" Behold, he comes !"   And moving hastily

She knelt upon her litter, raised above

The surging crowd, amid the tossing boughs

Of feathery palms.   Her eager eyes she bent

Upon the coming form.   Her hands she clasped

Above her bosom, seeking to hold down
Its quick, tumultuous throbbings.   And he saw !
Jesus of Nazareth saw the Magdalene !
The eye that loved the beauty of the flowers
Rested upon that flower-like face.   His look,
Piercing and puissant, clove that pearly breast
And saw the struggling human soul within
That blindly yearned for purity and love.
He saw her past, he knew her as she was,
And a divine compassion stirred his heart.
A look of mournful pity gave response
To her imploring eyes.   So passed he on,
And the great multitude closed round his form
And followed him toward the city gate.

X.

She did not weep, she did not cowering hide
Her face within her hands as she had feared
To do, remembering Probus' cruel words,
Beneath the Prophet's look of stern rebuke.

A strength undreamed of, from the Saviour's gaze

Flowed in upon her heart.   She felt a new

Transforming power move within her soul,

Which drew her on she knew not how, yet felt

That she must follow the great Prophet's steps :

There was the answer to her questionings !

But as her servants turned to bear her thence

From 'neath the shadowy olive, and she bent

Her lingering glance upon the green-strewn way

Where she the form of Jesus had beheld,

His look of mournful meaning smote upon

Her memory with sudden, vivid flash.

"What had those godlike eyes descried in her

That brought such depth of pity to their gaze ?

Had not the priests oft told her she was fair,

Fairest of Aphrodite's favourites ?

Had she not all that life and youth could give ?

What did she lack?   And yet he pitied her !

Had that all-piercing ken beheld the bar

Raised by that mystic holiness ?   What was

That haunting holiness?   It was perchance
Something she yet might win !"   And gladdening hope
Rose in the bosom of the Magdalene,
Sweet mingling with the deep and forceful want
That filled her soul with its imperious need,
As 'mid the hurrying of the eager crowd
Toward the massy gate she followed 'neath
Her canopy slow waving to and fro
In cadence with her bearers' measured tread,
While far above, the golden sunset sky
Bright with a radiance of new beauty shone.

XI.

And so they bore her to her stately home,
White gleaming 'mid its deep embowered shade
Of graceful cypresses and tufted palms.
As in a dream, she crossed the echoing hall
Circled by statues with unsleeping life,
And half unconsciously, she glided on
Across the polished floors of precious stone

Which mirrored her fair form and azure robes,

Until she neared the rich embroidered folds

That curtained deep her guarded chamber door.

But there she seemed to wake. Abrupt she paused,

Sudden drew back, and with a sign forbade

The waiting slave who ready stood to part

Those draperies; then turning to a stair

That upward led to the broad terraced roof,

She sought the solitude and stillness where,

Uplifted o'er the city's hum of life,

Fragrant and hushed, a little garden lay.

Beneath its sheltering vault high arched from shafts

Of slender, sculptured stone, a fountain played

That tossed its diamond sparkles in the air,

Besprinkling dew upon the quivering shrubs

And starry flowers that around it bent.

This was her favourite haunt, here would she muse

Long, silent hours by the cool fountain's brink,

With vibrant touch her ivory lyre would sound,

And sing the odes learnt in a far-off land.

XII.

Soon as her sandalled feet had pressed the moss

That carpeted that high, secluded spot,

To meet her coming a gazelle sprang forth,

Its liquid eyes with welcome shining bright,

While from the latticed cages placed around

Arose a joyous tumult of glad calls,

And sound of fluttering wings' impatient beat,

As all the little minstrels sought to catch

The gentle eye and ear of her they loved.

Their love was precious to her thirsting heart,

Forlorn and lonely in its gilded lot;

It had the power to win her from the thoughts

Rising in new-born majesty within

Her dimly wakening soul. With childlike smile

She oped their tiny gates: they circled round

The golden tresses of her graceful head,

Then perched upon her dimpled shoulders bare,

And nestled in her soft enfolding arms,

Until their evening greeting was fulfilled,

And in their airy homes they peaceful slept.

While she, reclining on a marble chair,

Her smooth cheek resting on her velvet hand,

The shy gazelle close couching by her side,

Leaned, gazing forth upon the deepening sky

With eyes that saw alone the Master's face.

Her past had faded utterly away,

And of the present knew she only this,

That Jesus silent called her life to him

With summons inarticulate, yet deep

Resounding in her soul.

XIII.

A light step broke

The silence, and a fair Athenian boy

With garland decked, advanced and bending low

Craved humbly that the banquet might no more

Await her coming; for her lordly guests

Impatient of her absence, marvelled loud,

No greeting from their hostess to receive.
Slow to her feet she rose, and gazed around
As seeking for the sense of words that strange
And void of meaning sounded on her ear.
Then through her frame a deep, long shiver ran:
The Prophet's face had vanished, and she was
Again that Mary, called the Magdalene.
But 'neath that consciousness she felt a will
That stronger than her own, constrained her words,
Charging her servants with attentive care
And courtesy to minister unto
Her guests, while she in solitude remained.
In wondering thought the graceful Grecian youth
Turned on his errand.   As his lithe form passed
Noiseless away, she called her constant guard,
The gold-girt Nubian, and mission gave
To learn where Jesus tarried for the night.
One only thought she had, to seek for him.
A strange mysterious instinct bore her on,
Awful yet sweet compulsion of her soul.

XIV.

As the moon rose, through a dark postern gate,

Leaving the sound of revelry and song

That from within her flower-strewn banquet hall

Streamed loud and fitful, forth the Magdalene,

Close followed by a band of armèd slaves

Led by the Nubian, passed into the gloom

That wrapt the city's bound.   A shrouding veil

Concealed her golden hair and vesture rich.

The tender feet that ne'er before had trode

The common street, now meekly tracked their way

Across the broken and disjointed paths

That led her at the last unto a long

And lowly building raised against the wall,

Hard by the space where the Great Temple reared

Its shining roof into the moonlit sky.

But all was hushed and still : the close-barred gate

And narrow windows blank and stirless showed

E

In that mute hour.   Entrance she dared not crave.
What claim had she to urge importunate
Her unknown presence on that wondrous One,
The Jewish Prophet-King?   With throbbing breast
She stood incredulous.   It could not be
That she had sought in vain !   That inner voice
Which called her forth, no mockery had proved !
It was no daemon summons from the dread
And shivering confines of the nether world
Had lured her from her home !   But as still lapsed
The leaden moments, and no sound within
Gave witness of the presence of that One
Whose pitying glance she came once more to meet,
A bitter wave of disappointment chill
Rose and benumbed her heart.   Her yearning hopes,
Quivering and bruised, sank down : their life died out
In sharp and shuddering pain.   A dumb despair
Crept, crushing every struggling thought within.
Anguished she turned her faint, reluctant steps
To leave the lonely and deserted spot,

When rising softly in rich-blended tone

Of human pathos and of heaven-born might,

A solemn.canticle of prayer and praise

Swelled on the midnight hush.   A strain it was

Such as the listening stars have never heard

Again since that last eve when Jesus' voice

* Intoned the hymn his followers upraised.

Deep and more deep the waves sonorous flowed,

Full and more full they poured upon her ear :

They bore her on their harmony sublime

Upward, still upward, till amid the stars

Her spirit seemed to float.   A peace profound,

A lofty calm, a fervent joy, instilled

Through all her being ; and a strength undreamed,

Mighty and forceful, held her soul within

Its clasp majestic ; while upon her breathed

Compassionate, a tenderness divine.

* Matthew xxvi. 30.   Mark xiv. 26.

XV.

That strain unearthly set her spirit free :
A sacred love flamed upward in her breast.
All ignorant she stood, yet to her heart
The gates of Heaven opened, ere her mind
Had trode the first steps of the holy way
Of wisdom and of truth.   A portent high
Of saving love had snatched her from the life
She knew not how to hate.   She gazed above
With unveiled head thrown back.   Her bosom heaved,
Tears slowly welling stole adown her cheeks,
And lifting up her arms she suppliant stood,
Invoking silently the Unknown God.

XVI.

As though retiring upward to the sky,
The sounds majestic died upon her ear,
And silence softly sank on all around ;
Yet still the harp-strings of her being thrilled,

Vibrating with a new, mysterious sense,

Sweet, awful dawning of the spirit life !

Solemn and bright the golden moon shone down,

And from the starry depths a splendour gleamed

Like distant waving of celestial wings,

As to the alien shelter of her home,

Her wondering soul inorbed with heavenly light,

The Magdalene, Christ's miracle, returned.

XVII.

And ever from that day, where Jesus taught,

In the still coolness of the early dawn,

Standing within the crowded market-place

Amid the simple country folk who brought

The bright-hued products of their narrow lands ;

The hardy fishermen who from the shores

Of deep blue lakes had borne their glistening spoils ;

The shepherds who the younglings of the flock

Reluctantly had led from dewy meads ;

While all, close gathered, reverently heard

Wise speech of gentle counsel from his lips;

There, standing on the farthest verge, was seen

A youthful figure wrapt in shrouding veil

And sweeping robes of dark and shadowy fold,

Still followed by a swarthy Nubian slave,

Who in a silver leash a leopard led.

XVIII.

When in the scorching noon, beneath the shade

Of the Great Temple's lofty portico,

Its vistas opening into spacious courts

Magnificent with cedar-work and gold,

And hung with wondrous glowing draperies

Of ruddy crimson and resplendent blue,

Filled with the pilgrims who from morn till night

Passed ceaselessly toward the Holy Place

Of their stern country's fierce and ancient faith;

His solemn tones of urgent warning rang:

Amid the host of scowling Pharisees

Wearing broad-bordered garments, jealous Scribes,

And subtle Doctors of the Law, who sought

With cunning questions and insidious art

To draw some fatal sentence from his lips

Which, falsely commented, might set aflame

The sleeping fury of the fiery Jews,

Giving pretext to stone him where he stood;

There, on the border of the curious throng

That pressed to trap him in his speech, or shrunk

Crouching beneath his malediction stern,

The scathing rain of his indignant words,

Was ever seen that mute and listening form.

XIX.

When the cool softness of the evening fell,

As 'mid the people Jesus walked abroad,

And crowding round him came the helpless ones,

The blind, the sick, the maimed, brought to his feet

By those who loved them, that the Prophet might

With powerful word restore them to their arms

Made whole again, and healèd of their hurt;

Or when he trode through dark and winding lanes,
Through foul and noisome corners, stifling courts,
Wherever poverty and wretchedness
Dragged out the slow, sad torment of their days,
And ignorance and stupid blindness wrought
Their close-drawn web to bind the spirit's eyes,
And untaught bigotry proclaimed the Law
That daily ground them to the earth as just,
And greed rapacious sought to snare the poor
Still poorer than itself, and mourners wept
Disconsolate alone, and conscience strove
With choking sense of sin, and weary toil
Sought feverish for rest; still followed him,
The shadow of that silent neophyte.

XX.

As tender mother teaches little child
By simple story, that its feeble thought
Along the pictured path of wisdom may
With tottering steps be gently guided on

Until it reach at last the distant heights

Whence the great sea of truth shall meet its eye ;

So Jesus taught the people, leading on

Their minds toward his truth by flowery ways

Of parable, of simple, childlike tales,

To feed the growing want that held them hushed

Hearkening in reverence to his ministering,

That ministry of love.   The Magdalene,

Childlike in ignorance, her thought athirst

For that diviner knowledge which the priests

Had never taught in her far-distant home,

Stood earnest listening to the words that fell

From the firm lips of Jesus.   Day by day

They sank upon her heart like blessed rain,

Calling the secret powers that lay within

Deep buried, forth to beauty and to life.

And as the world of spirit to her eye

Dawned in its dim-seen majesty of light,

Slowly her conscience roused ; until there came,

Supreme and awful, that awakening flash

When by illumination dread, distinct,

She saw the image of that holiness

She sought with deepest craving to behold.

With high translated vision she discerned

The mirror of her past, and knew herself

The desecrated temple of a soul !

XXI.

Dim sank the twilight o'er the busy street

Whereon a lordly mansion raised its front,

The home of a rich Pharisee.   A crowd

Of humble poor stood gathered at the gate

Waiting to see the coming forth of him

Who all the city stirred ; for Jesus sate

At meat within the high-born ruler's house.

And as they stood and watched, a youthful form,

Shrouded and veiled, passed slow athwart the throng,

Bearing a vase of alabaster, carved,

And set with stones of price.   She neared the gate

And asked for entrance ; and the servants looked

Upon the precious vase, and passage made

For her who came with such resplendent gift.

XXII.

Fair was the spacious room, and graced with all

That wealth could buy or luxury devise.

Frescoes of Grecian art adorned the walls,

On Roman couches richly cushioned o'er

The guests reclined around the lavish board ;

Silent they lay, the while their cold eyes turned

With curious question in their haughty look

Upon one form the ruler's place beside,

Which rested wearily as though the day

Of labour had its strength full sorely tried.

Low whispering among themselves the train

Of debtors and of bondmen passed around,

And eager watched for word that yet might come

From him they knew the dauntless friend of all

The poor and the oppressed, the hated foe

Of their relentless master and his sect.

XXIII.

Awhile that shrouded form stood motionless
Within the portal of the long-roofed hall,
Trembling and silent; then she forward moved ;
With faltering steps until she reached the couch
Where Jesus lay reclined.   Upon her knees
She sank beside his feet; her veil fell back,
And all beheld the golden waving hair,
The lovely face of Mary Magdalene.
She oped the vase; its costly perfume filled
The spacious room; she bent above those feet
Fevered with loving toil.   Her lips she pressed
With timid touch upon them, and the while
She bathed them with her warm, fast-flowing tears,
Then wiped them with the gold of her long hair,
Still kissing them, as if that act of love
Were all of hope the earth contained for her.
Then from the open vase she ointment poured
Of priceless worth upon them, sobbing deep

As one whose heart is breaking in its pain.

And Jesus turned his eyes and saw the look

Of scornful wonder running round the board,

And heard the inner echo of their thoughts ;

And spake to him, the ruler of the feast,

"Simon, somewhat to say to thee I have."

He coldly answered, "Master, say thou on."

XXIV.

Each sound was stilled, and every breath was hushed

As Jesus raised his deep, vibrating voice

And said, "There was a certain creditor

Who had two debtors ; one to him did owe

Five hundred pence, fifty the other owed :

And seeing that they nothing had to pay,

He freely both forgave.   Now tell me which

Of those whom he forgave will love him most?"

The ruler answered with contemptuous smile,

"He whom he most forgave."   And Jesus said,

"Most rightly hast thou judged."   Then stretching forth

His hand toward Magdalene, he slowly spoke;
"Seest thou this woman?   When within thine house
I came, thou gav'st no water for my feet;
But she has washed my feet with rain of tears,
And wiped them with her hair.   No greeting kiss
Thou gavest me; but she has ceasèd not
To kiss my feet.   No oil thou brought'st to pour
Upon my head; but she upon my feet
Has poured out ointment.   Wherefore do I say
Her sins, and they are many, are forgiven,
For she has lovèd much."   He turned and looked
On her that was a sinner, as she knelt
With low bowed head and golden streaming hair,
Veiling the shame-struck anguish of her face
From the stern gaze of hostile eyes, all bent
Upon her shrinking form; and in a voice
Of tender, yearning pity, Jesus said,
"Woman, thou art forgiven; go in peace!"

Part Third.

I.

PORTENTOUS, heavy with thick, thunderous gloom,

Dark clouds the heavens shrouded on that day,

When high upon his cross God's chosen One

Was raised to die by impious hands of men.

Against the lurid sky his head stood forth

Crowned with sharp thorns in bitter sign of scorn.

Those gracious hands that healed the helpless sick,

Gave sight unto the blind, now bruised and torn,

Were nailed with iron spikes unto the wood

Which deep stained drank their blood.   Those earnest feet

That brought the beauty of glad tidings, pierced
With anguished wounds, distilled slow dropping gore.
Slowly its life was ebbing from his frame,
Yet still that mighty heart retained its love,
That massive brain its strength.　With steadfast eyes
Gazing above, he prayed those words divine,
" Father, forgive : they know not what they do !"

II.

And at the sound the seething crowd grew still :
The angry cries of fierce, vindictive hate,
The mocking jeers, the scoffing taunts, were hushed.
A chill and shuddering awe sank deep within
Those hot and furious hearts ; a human pang
Wrung with its unaccustomed thrill those breasts
Of bigots and of outcasts, flocked to see
The lingering torments of the Prophet's death ;
And with a sudden fear they turned away,
Smiting their breasts, and left him there alone.

III.

A group of women on that bleak hill-side

All through the dreadful day had stood and watched ;

While the tumultuous surging of the crowd

Rising and falling round that fearful cross

Forbade them to approach.   But now they came,

Pallid and weeping, and beside his feet

With choking sobs they took their faithful stand.

Yet one was there who neither sobbed nor shrank,

Favoured of God, the Mother of the Lord.

She stood with steadfast face and look sublime :

On her uplifted brow a lambent light

Descended from the dark and lurid sky,

As though her sight had pierced the deep-massed clouds,

Cleaving a passage for celestial rays.

Within her eyes prophetic vision spoke,

She saw the full completion of that day.

The Past, the Present, and the Future, kept

Their watch beside her through those hours supreme ;

F

Voices swept onward from all coming time,

And heralded Creation's Mystery

To her expanding soul.   So stood she there,

Uplifted glorious o'er bereavement, raised

By inspiration high above all pain ;

Stronger than Grief, more resolute than Death,

The Mighty Mother of a Son Divine.

IV.

And with her came the ghost of Magdalene,

For such it seemed.   No tears her dry eyes shed ;

Dilated with unutterable woe

They straining gazed on that majestic face

Which gave its silent greeting to his friends

Even in that dread hour.   Her pallid lips,

Parted with horror, sent their struggling breath

In heavy gasps ; her hands, convulsive clenched,

Were pressed upon her forehead, as to chain

The agony of frenzied thought within.

" The Saviour of mankind, God's Holy One,

   Was dying there in torture on the cross !"

   Nought else her mind could seize, nought else she knew

   Within the darkling boundaries of space.

   Each pang he felt her aching sense returned ;

   Each fainting groan that told the end was near

   Lessened the pulse within her sinking frame :

   And when his death-cry sounded on her ear,

   And he, her soul's Redeemer, bowed his head

   And breathed forth his pure life, thick darkness swept

   Its pall about her, and she senseless fell

   Prone on the stony earth, in mercy snatched

   From grief which woman never knew before.

V.

The anguish of the Sabbath day had throbbed

Through its dark hours of midnight, and was come

The first day of the week, the third from that

Which saw the Saviour die.   The early morn

Broke o'er the garden where his form was laid

In silence, and in secrecy and tears,

To rest from anguish in its close-sealed tomb.

Deserted by all else, one mourner there

Beside that rifled couch of stone kept watch,

Weeping, while in her clasping hand she held

The crown of thorns, the all that now remained

To her of him.   'Twas Mary Magdalene.

Sobbing, she prest her shuddering lips to those

Keen points stained cruel crimson with his blood ;

She held them to her quivering breast, nor thought

To heed the sharp pain of their pointed darts :

'Twas all she had of him, and he was dead !

VI.

She stood and watched in the chill twilight drear,

While hushed the garden lay in morn's repose ;

The cold gray sky as yet revealed no sign

Of rose clouds welcoming the burst of day.

She stood and wept, while aching memory traced

Her life since o'er her bended head those words

Had sounded from his deep and pitying voice,
" Woman, thou art forgiven ; go in peace !"
All had she sold of that which she possessed,
To give unto the poor.   Her feet had trode
Since then, alone the gloomy precincts where
Disease and want stretched out their starving hands ;
Or, following her Master's steps, had gone
Forth 'mid his band of humble friends, to hear
His teachings to the people.   And now all
Was ended.   On the agonising cross
Her eyes had seen him die ; her ears had heard
His last expiring groan.   He who had saved
Her life from sin, had opened to her soul
The way of truth and peace and holiness,
Jesus was dead, and she was desolate !

VII.

And while she wept, upon her consciousness
A form dawned slowly, standing near to her.
Mist-veiled by tears, her blinded eyes she turned

Upon that form, nor knew whom she beheld.

And the Lord spoke to her thus mourning sore ;

" Woman, why weepest thou ?" he gently said ;

" Whom seekest thou ?" And still her ears the while

Throbbing in cadence with her sobs, knew not

The voice of him who spoke. With pleading prayer,

Heart-broken and imploring, she replied,

" Oh, Sir, if thou indeed have borne him hence,

Tell me where thou hast laid him, and I will

Take him away." And Jesus looked upon

That loving, lovely face, and said to her,

" Mary !" And sudden recognition came.

The echoing heavens opened and did bow

Themselves in light transcendent at the word !

In transport of thanksgiving love she kneeled,

And reaching forth her glad, entreating hands

Her soul sent up its worship in the cry,

" Master, my Master !" Jesus drew not back,

But said unto her, " Touch me not, for I

Am not ascended to my Father's home.

This spiritual body which thou seest

May suffer not approach of mortal hands.—

Now listen to my words.   To thee I come.

Thee have I chosen as my messenger.

Thy lips shall be the first to tell mankind

That I, Christ Jesus crucified, still live.

Go thou from me unto my brethren.   Say

Unto them, I ascend unto my God,

And to my Father : to your God I rise,

And to your Father !   Go and bear my words."

And looking on her as she knelt, her face

Filled with the tender transport of the pure

And sacred adoration of her heart,

Radiant with glory borrowed from the skies,

The Saviour's gaze breathed forth celestial love :

Then slow dissolving into viewless air

His form majestic vanished from her sight.

VIII.

And she fulfilled that sacred last behest ;

His messenger, appointed to proclaim

His resurrection to the waiting world.

She bore unto the sad remorseful band

Of those who had forsaken him, their Lord,

His greeting of forgiving love sublime

E'er he ascended to his God and theirs :

And then we know no more.   We know but this,

When Jesus Christ was risen from the dead

He first appeared to Mary Magdalene.

THE END.

Printed by R. & R. CLARK, *Edinburgh.*